www.fast-print.net/store.php

A Trial for Iris

Copyright © Gregor Girvan 2013

A catalogue record for this book is available from the British Library

ISBN 978-178035-666-2

First published 2013 by
FASTPRINT PUBLISHING
Peterborough, England.

Bear words

groddle – human (man or woman)

grout – bad human

A New Day

Iris opened her eyes and smiled. Without a moment's thought she jumped up, skipped into the bathroom and made for the mirror. Her fur looked neat and shiny and after a quick wash she decided that all that was needed was the magic crayon or lipstick as groddles called it. A few minutes later she made her way to the front door to see if there was any mail. Lying on the mat was a letter. She picked it up and saw it had foreign stamps and was addressed to her. Iris shook with excitement, could this be the news that she had longed for?

On the other side of the world, a different kind of bear stirred. With something of a long growl, Jock slowly climbed out of bed.

He shuffled into the bathroom and peered in the mirror. Looking back, he saw a grumpy face. Jock didn't feel miserable but he sighed, thinking that perhaps his reflection didn't lie. He pondered a little then shook out his fur, gave himself a little talking to and decided to be positive, just like his team mate, Chi. Next week football training would start and he was determined to play well and show he could have fun, just like the rest of The Ready Bears.

Back in South America, Iris peeled open the letter. It was from The Ready Bears and yes... fantastic news, the football club wanted her to come for a trial. Filled with excitement, she ran into the kitchen to share the good news with her mum who cried with delight and hugged her tightly. For a couple of minutes the embrace continued. This was a proper bear hug unlike the copycat sort that groddles had adopted.

After the excitement died down, Iris' mum decided to have a chat with her daughter.

'You've seen a few groddles in the past' she remarked.

Iris looked back quizzically.

'Well now you're going to come into contact with quite a lot of them. You must take care because whilst most are good, there are a few that are bad... the grouts.

They can steal, destroy our habitat, harm our animal neighbours and even other groddles. You won't recognise them but always remember - there could be grout about'

Iris felt a bit uneasy. She knew groddles had flat faces and their lack of hair made them look silly but up till now she had just thought of them as football fans. She would have to remember her mum's words.

Iris Gets a Scare

A week later, Iris stepped down from the plane. It was the first time she had been away from home. The sun was shining and it was warmer than she had imagined. As she passed through the airport she thought about why she had come to Scotland. It was to follow her dream and to play football for The Ready Bears.

She picked up her bags and followed the signs to the taxi rank where a big groddle came towards her. He was shouting into a mobile phone and waving his arms about. Iris looked cautiously at him, what if this was a grout? Iris suddenly felt cold and started to shiver. The groddle's mobile began to expand but try though he may, he couldn't let it go. The mobile phone became alive and grew fangs, worms appeared on it's head and purple saliva streamed from it's mouth. With a thunderous noise the mobile began to devour the groddle. Iris felt her mouth drop in disbelief as the groddle slowly disappeared.

Miraculously the horrible sight disappeared. What had happened? No one else seemed to notice that anything had occurred. Iris waited nervously at the taxi rank.

A Funny Language

When she was at the front of the taxi queue, Iris heard a voice

"whur tae?" [where to?]

Iris had studied English for five years and felt she could speak it well but the taxi driver's words just left her confused so she smiled and replied

"pardon?"

"Where ur ye goin?" [where are you going?]

said the groddle. Iris still didn't understand and continued to look puzzled so the taxi driver raised his voice and asked, very slowly

"Whur tae, hotel maybe?"

Now there was a word that Iris did recognise, so she quickly replied

"yes, Hotel Hideaway please"

The groddle nodded, picked up her bags and put them in the boot of the taxi.

All the way to the hotel, the taxi driver chatted away in his heavy Scottish accent. Iris smiled and nodded her head when she thought it best to agree and by the time they arrived at the hotel, they seemed like best of friends. As they parted, the groddle shouted

"hae a gid stay" [have a good stay]

Iris still didn't understand but she smiled and waved goodbye.

In her room, she unpacked her bags and lay on the bed thinking about what had happened. Why had the groddle disappeared in such a horrific way and why had everything been fine with the taxi driver? Iris decided to think about tomorrow. A trial with The Ready Bears was a great opportunity but could she be the first female to play for a top football team? Her head spun as she thought about whether she'd be good enough but it had been a very long day and she soon drifted off to sleep.

Iris Feels Uneasy

The next day, Iris rose early and followed the directions to the training ground. As she entered the dressing room, she noticed a plaque on the wall which said

The Club Code
Play fair, you're a Ready Bear
Don't dive, cheats won't thrive
Respect the ref. he's not deaf
Don't waste time, it's a crime

Underneath the words someone had scribbled

No trumping or you'll get a thumping!

Iris thought this was very rude but she knew from her team mates back home that males seemed to have a fascination with passing wind. Once again, she wondered if she'd be accepted.

Suddenly, the door opened and a rather serious looking brown bear entered. Jock looked Iris up and down and grunted
    "You're sitting on my seat"

Iris apologised and shuffled down the bench to a different spot.

Soon the dressing room had filled up and Iris noticed that there were all sorts of bears. She soon realised however that she was the only spectacled bear and... she was the only female.

Another brown bear approached her and said something but he sounded just like the taxi driver. Iris smiled and nodded her head hoping it would be an opportunity to make a friend. This time however it didn't work, the brown bear looked annoyed, turned his back and walked away. A few minutes passed and Iris began to feel uneasy. She knew the trial would be difficult but if her team mates didn't like her, how would she ever fit in?

A loud voice filled the room.

"OK, listen up"

It was the coach, Luigi. Iris had read a lot about The Ready Bears coach and she hoped he'd give her a fair chance. He continued

"Look on the notice board and see what team you're in. We've got a player on trial with us today, her name is Iris and she's from Venezuela. Consider her a team mate but no special treatment because she's female."

Iris felt herself go red at the mention of her name and she looked towards the floor in embarrassment. Again she doubted herself, would her shyness be mistaken for weakness? If she'd looked up however, she would have seen that Jock was looking at her with a friendly smile.

The Trial

Ten minutes later the game began and Iris was in the red team. Nothing much happened for a few minutes when suddenly the ball passed in front of her. She set off in hot pursuit but just as she reached it, a leg appeared and kicked the ball away. Iris tumbled over the outstretched leg and rolled over on the ground. She stayed still for a few moments, then held her leg before looking up to see the tackler standing over her. It was Chi, a panda and the captain of the Ready Bears.

"We don't do that"
said the panda before walking away.

Iris rose to her feet and remembered the Code. It was clear that the panda had thought she was pretending to be injured. Iris certainly didn't consider herself to be a cheat as she was just doing what previous coaches had told her to do. She ran back to her position, worried that she may have offended her team mates. Soon after, the blue team scored and for the rest of the first half, Iris contributed very little.

At the interval, Iris walked slowly from the field. She hadn't played well and all she seemed to have done today was upset the other bears. She sat alone and felt like giving up. A few minutes later she noticed that someone had sat down beside her. It was Luigi. The coach looked at her and said

"I've had good reports from my friend in Venezuela. He says you're very skilful and a fine player."

And putting his arm around her shoulder, he smiled and added

"And he's never been wrong."

Iris took to the field for the second half and thought about what the coach had said. It wasn't long before she was in the action. She took a pass from the grumpy looking bear, dribbled past two defenders and sent a great cross into the centre.

The ball was met by a teammate who headed the ball powerfully into the net. Iris continued to play well and as full time approached she received another good pass from the grumpy bear. Without hesitation she sent a powerful shot into the top of the net. Her team mates cheered and rushed over to congratulate her. Ten minutes later, the game ended and the red team had won 2 – 1.

Does Iris Make The Team?

Making her way back to the changing room, Iris wondered if she'd done enough to convince the coach. As she walked in, the grumpy brown bear stood up and offered her his paw saying

"My name's Jock, and you can have my seat"

Iris smiled and accepted the paw. She sat down and waited. Two minutes later, a stern looking Luigi approached her.

Iris was convinced it would be bad news. Luigi asked

"Your plane ticket, was it for a return journey?"

"Well yes" Iris replied

"I've got some bad news" continued Luigi "you've wasted your money then"

at first Iris didn't understand what the coach meant but as Jock shouted out

"'We've got a new team mate"

she realised that she had been accepted. With great excitement, she leapt to her feet with delight and was quickly joined by the brown bear who had spoken to her earlier. He shouted

"'I'm Jimmy and in Scotland we celebrate like this"

Iris watched as Jimmy flung his arms in the air, twirled round and round and shrieked like a mad bear. Jock joined in, clapping his paws and stamping his feet whilst the other bears cheered them along.

Iris stood back, watched the mayhem and smiled. Today her dream had come true and in front of her were her new family, The Ready Bears.

Iris Realises What's Happening

As they left the changing room, Jock was the last to leave. He glanced at his reflection in the mirror – and yes, there was the faint glimmer of a smile on his face. What had changed he thought to himself; was it his attitude today or had it been the affect of a certain new arrival? He wasn't sure why but he felt a sudden spring in his step... a whole new world was opening up for him.

Iris had made her way back towards the hotel. She reflected on how glad she was to have made the team but hoped she'd never have to experience again what happened at the airport. Had it been a grout she'd encountered and had she caused him to disappear so horribly?

Then she turned a corner and was shocked to see a large grout towering over a frail groddle and trying to steal her handbag. The attacker saw Iris appearing and looked guiltily towards her. Iris felt cold and started to shiver. The handbag, clutched by the grout, started to expand... Iris felt her heart racing... watching in horror she realised the power she possessed.

The Future

Will Iris and Jock become good friends?
Are the Bears good enough to beat
teams of lions and tigers?
How will Iris use her power?

www.thereadybears.com